Stripey Socks

Written by
Stephen Rickard

See my socks.
My socks are yellow.

See my socks.
My socks are white.

See my socks.

My socks are green.

See my socks.
My socks are pink.

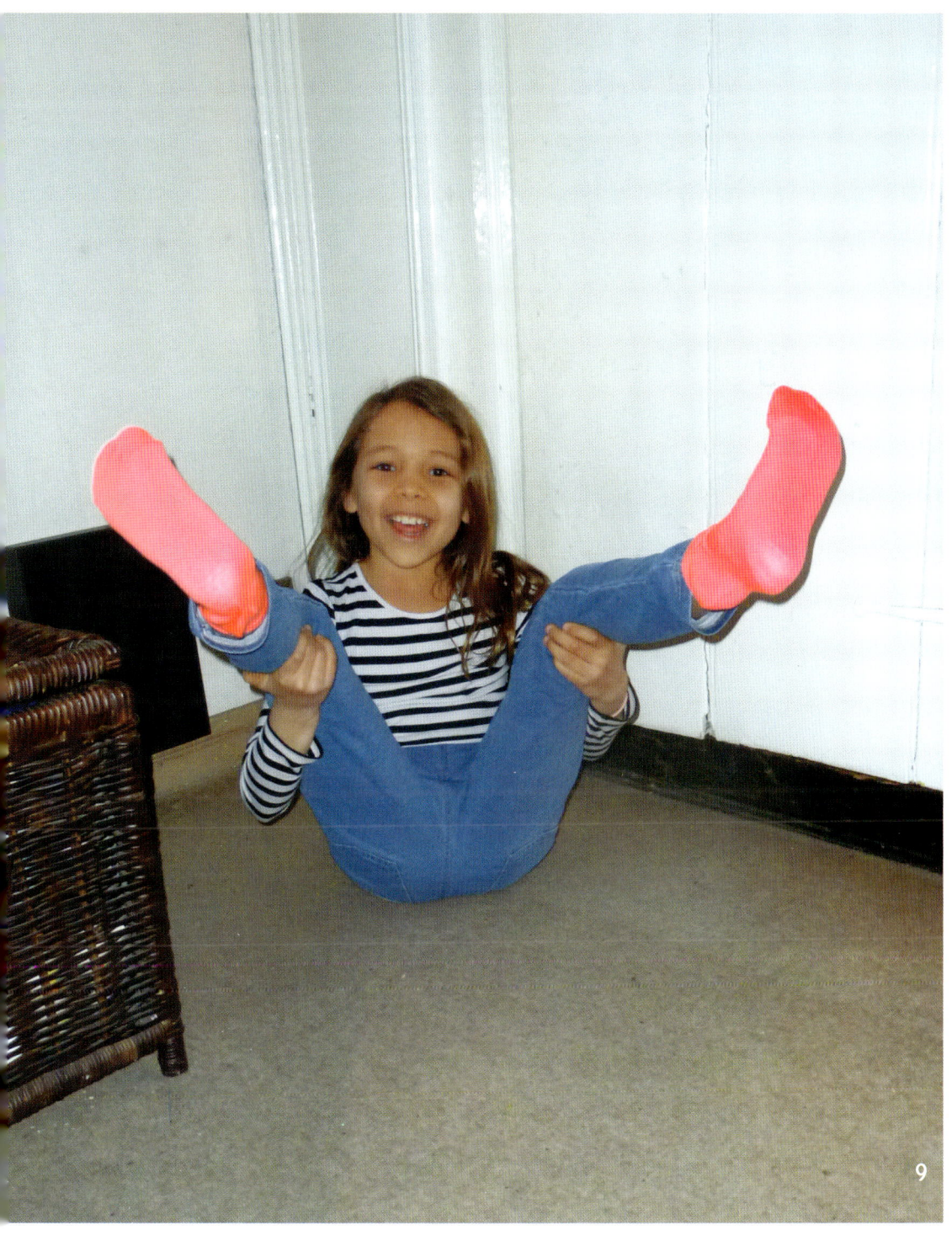

See my socks.

My socks are pink and green and white.

My socks are stripey.

See the yellow
and the white
and the green
and the pink
and the stripey socks.